# THE CALLED
# STORM

# THE CALLED STORM

E.M. COLE

**PALMETTO**
PUBLISHING
Charleston, SC
www.PalmettoPublishing.com

Copyright © 2024 by E.M. Cole

All rights reserved

No portion of this book may be reproduced, stored in a retrieval system, or transmitted in any form by any means—electronic, mechanical, photocopy, recording, or other—except for brief quotations in printed reviews, without prior permission of the author.

Hardcover ISBN: 9798822958067
Paperback ISBN: 9798822958050
eBook ISBN: 9798822958074

# CONTENTS

| | | |
|---|---|---:|
| PROLOGUE | | VII |
| CHAPTER 1: | SETTING THE SCENE | 1 |
| CHAPTER 2: | THE BOAT OUTING | 5 |
| CHAPTER 3: | THE STORM | 8 |
| CHAPTER 4: | WHAT CAME AFTER THE STORM? | 10 |
| CHAPTER 5: | SURVIVAL | 12 |
| CHAPTER 6: | HALLUCINATIONS & THE RESCUE | 22 |
| CHAPTER 7: | THE RETURN | 26 |
| CHAPTER 8: | STUCK IN THE PAST | 32 |
| CHAPTER 9: | NEW BEGINNINGS | 41 |
| CHAPTER 10: | HIDDEN GAMES | 46 |
| CHAPTER 11: | WHAT DO TERNS TASTE LIKE? | 50 |
| CHAPTER 12: | LOOSE ENDS | 54 |
| CHAPTER 13: | THE FINAL DINNER | 58 |
| CHAPTER 14: | THE STORM | 62 |

# PROLOGUE

John awoke to the sensation of being dragged across coarse sand, the rhythmic pull on his life jacket sending twinges of pain through his body. The sting in his left leg intensified as he became more aware of his surroundings. The last thing he remembered was the boat crashing, the roaring waves swallowing them whole. Now, he found himself on a beach, drenched and disoriented.

As he opened his eyes, John took in the sight of a shadowy figure pulling him away from the water's edge. The sun hung low in the sky, casting long shadows across the deserted island. The man beside him wore tattered clothes, and his face was obscured by unruly, salt-soaked hair.

"Easy there," the man grunted, glancing back at John. "You took a nasty hit to the leg. We need to get you patched up."

John's mind was a foggy haze of confusion, but he managed to piece together the situation. He and Jake were the only survivors. The crash, the storm—they were still fresh in his memory.

"Where are we?" John croaked, his throat dry and scratchy.

"Lost in the middle of nowhere," the man replied cryptically. "But we'll talk more once you're in better shape. Can you walk?"

With the man's help, John struggled to his feet, wincing at the pain shooting through his leg. As he limped away from the shore, he stole a glance at the wrecked boat, battered and broken against the rocks.

# SETTING THE SCENE

The coastal town of Ternery embraced the Salters with open arms, becoming a haven for John, Sara, and their lively son, Matt. The family's house, perched on the edge of the harbor, resonated with the echoes of laughter and the warmth of shared moments. It was a small home, its walls adorned with photos capturing the essence of a life well-lived.

The aroma of fresh sea air wafted through the open windows as John, a man with salt-and-pepper hair that spoke of countless adventures, stood on the porch overlooking the harbor. Sara, the heart of their home, bustling around in the kitchen with a warm smile and a twinkle in her eye, prepared a picnic basket. Their son, Matt, a bundle of energy, bounced around with eagerness, excited about the day's impending adventure.

"John, don't forget the sunscreen," Sara called from the kitchen, handing him a thermos of coffee. "We don't want anyone turning into a lobster today."

John chuckled, taking the thermos. "I'll make sure we're all properly protected, Captain," he said, a term of endearment he often used for Sara. The coastal breeze tousled Matt's hair as he darted back and forth, a sea sprite in the making.

Down the street, the Salter family shared a close-knit relationship with Jake, their neighbor. Jake, a wiry man with a perpetual grin and a shared zest for adventure, was an inseparable part of their daily lives. The connection between the families went beyond mere neighborly camaraderie; it was a bond forged in the crucible of shared joys and sorrows.

As John prepared the boat for the impromptu outing, the wooden dock extending from their backyard became a stage for the unfolding adventure. The boat, a vessel weathered by the tides of time, held the promise of sunlit waves and the whisper of endless horizons. Sara donning a sea-blue scarf, moved gracefully between the kitchen and the dock, her eyes sparkling with a secret hidden beneath the surface.

"Jake, my man!" John called out, spotting his friend approaching. "Ready for a day at sea?"

Jake grinned, clapping John on the back. "Always, my friend. You know I'm up for an adventure."

The boat, christened "Sea Serenade," cast off, leaving the harbor behind as the Salter family and Jake settled in for a day of relaxation. The sun played hide-and-seek with the clouds, casting a golden glow over the waters. Matt excitedly shared his dreams for his upcoming 10th birthday.

"I want a pirate-themed party, Mom," he exclaimed, his eyes sparkling with imagination. "With a treasure hunt and everything!" Sara laughed, ruffling Matt's hair. "A pirate-themed party it is, then. We'll make it the best birthday ever."

As the boat glided through the gentle waves, the air was filled with laughter and the tantalizing aroma of a picnic lunch prepared by Sara. Amidst the joyous banter, however, Sara stole a glance at her phone, a device that held the key to the day's unforeseen twist.

The weather forecast flashed on the screen, predicting an approaching storm. Sara's gaze lingered on the ominous signs, and a calculated decision was made to keep this information concealed—a secret plan set in motion to turn an ordinary boat outing into an unforgettable adventure for Matt.

John Salter was not the average man you'd meet in a small town though.

With salt-and-pepper hair that hinted at the many tales etched into his past, John's rugged demeanor concealed a history of intrigue and high-stakes missions. Once upon a time, he had been a shadow, a phantom navigating the treacherous world of espionage as a spy for the Secret Service.

In the clandestine world of covert operations, John's skills were unparalleled. He was the man you called when the mission seemed impossible, the kind of operative who could blend into the shadows without leaving a trace. His past was a mosaic of classified information, each more dangerous than the last.

It was during one such mission that he crossed paths with Sara. She was the beacon of warmth in a world often draped in shadows. Her kindness and genuine nature were like a balm to John's hardened soul. As he navigated the complexities of the mission, Sara's unwavering support became his anchor, a reminder that goodness existed even in the darkest corners.

Sara, with her warm smile and the twinkle in her eye, was the perfect woman—a rare blend of strength and kindness. She stood by John during the most perilous moments of his life, offering solace and understanding. She became the light at the end of his covert tunnel, and their connection blossomed into something beyond the confines of a mission.

The decision to leave the secret service life behind wasn't an easy one for John. The adrenaline-fueled world of espionage had become second nature. But the desire for a different kind of life, a life with Sara, outweighed the life of shadows and secrets.

John transitioned to a quieter existence, leaving behind the cloak-and-dagger world for a more ordinary, yet fulfilling life. He found solace in odd jobs, embracing the simplicity of everyday tasks. The coastal town became their refuge, a place where John could rebuild his life with Sara by his side.

Eventually, John found stability in an unexpected place. A small company in town offered him the chance to utilize his skills in a different way. The world of database engineering became his new frontier, a far cry from the covert operations of his past. It was a quiet life, one that allowed John to focus on building a future with Sara.

The coastal town, once a mere backdrop to John's missions, transformed into the canvas on which he painted the chapters of a new beginning. The echo of waves against the shore became a lullaby, replacing the distant echoes of gunshots and whispered secrets.

And so, John Salter, the spy turned database engineer, embraced the ordinary. His past, though veiled in shadows, had shaped him into the man who found solace in the simple joys of life—a life that began with a chance meeting on a mission and evolved into a love story worthy of the quiet town by the sea.

# THE BOAT OUTING

The sun danced across the waves as the Sea Serenade cut through the sparkling waters, carrying John, Sara, Matt, and Jake on their much-anticipated boat outing. Laughter echoed off the boat's wooden deck as they boarded, their excitement through the roof in the salty breeze that tousled their hair.

With supplies neatly stowed away and life jackets securely fastened, they pushed off from the dock, the engine purring beneath them as they set out into the open sea. Matt, with his infectious grin and boundless energy, scampered around the deck, his laughter mingling with the gentle lapping of the waves against the hull.

"Isn't this just perfect?" Sara exclaimed, her eyes sparkling with joy as she leaned against the railing, taking in the panoramic view of the coastline stretching out before them. John nodded, a smile playing at the corners of his lips. "Absolutely, Sara. There's nowhere else I'd rather be than out here with you and Matt." Matt, overhearing his parents' conversation, bounded over with excitement. "Mom, Dad, can we go fishing? Please? I want to catch the biggest fish ever!" John chuckled, tousling Matt's hair affectionately. "Of course, buddy. We'll find the perfect spot and see if we can reel in a big one."

With Matt's enthusiasm leading the way, they set up their fishing gear and cast their lines into the depths below. As they whiled away the hours, Matt shared his plans for his upcoming birthday, his eyes sparkling with excitement at the thought of a pirate-themed party complete with treasure hunts and swashbuckling adventures. Sara listened attentively, her heart swelling with pride at her son's boundless imagination.

"Sounds like it's going to be the best birthday ever, Matt," Jake chimed in, his grin widening as he imagined the festivities.

But as the afternoon wore on, a subtle shift in the weather began to unfold. The once-clear sky was now covered by darkening clouds, and a cool breeze swept across the deck, carrying with it a hint of uncertainty.

John furrowed his brow, his gaze flickering up at the gathering storm clouds on the horizon. "Looks like the weather might be turning," he remarked, his voice tinged with concern.

Sara glanced at the darkening sky, a furrow of worry creasing her brow. "Do you think we should head back?" she asked, her gaze shifting between John and Jake.

But Jake waved off her concerns with a dismissive grin. "Ah, come on, Sara. It's probably just a passing shower. We'll be fine out here."

Emboldened by Jake's reassurance, they continued on their journey, the boat forging ahead through the increasingly choppy waters. Matt's laughter echoed off the waves as he regaled them with tales of daring adventures, his imagination soaring as high as the seagulls circling overhead.

But as the storm clouds gathered ominously overhead, a sense of unease settled over the group like a heavy blanket. The once-playful banter grew subdued, replaced by a tense silence punctuated only by the distant rumble of thunder.

John glanced at the horizon, his instincts warning him of the impending danger. "Maybe we should turn back," he suggested, his voice barely audible above the rising wind.

But Jake shook his head stubbornly, his gaze fixed on the distant shoreline. "We're already halfway there, John. We can't turn back now. Besides, what's a little rain to a group of seasoned sailors like us?"

Reluctantly, John listened, his concern tempered by Jake's confidence. But as the storm clouds loomed ever closer and the wind whipped around them with increasing ferocity, John couldn't shake the sinking feeling in the pit of his stomach.

Little did they know, their carefree boat outing was about to take a dark turn, plunging them into a harrowing ordeal that would test their courage, resilience, and the strength of their bonds.

# THE STORM

As the Sea Serenade battled against the growing waves and darkening skies, the once-idyllic boat outing descended into a frantic struggle for survival. The gentle breeze that had carried them out to sea now whipped around them with increasing ferocity, churning the waters into a frothy tempest.

Jake and John, their faces grim with determination, worked in tandem to navigate the treacherous waters. With each gust of wind and towering wave that crashed against the boat's hull, their efforts became more desperate, their adrenaline-fueled resolve the only thing keeping them afloat.

"We need to get the sails down, John!" Jake shouted over the howling wind, his voice barely audible above the roar of the storm.

John nodded, his jaw set in determination as he wrestled with the flapping sails. With every muscle strained to its limit, he fought against the raging elements, his hands numb with cold and exertion.

But just as they managed to secure the sails, disaster struck. With a sickening lurch, the boat's engine sputtered and died, leaving them at the mercy of the relentless storm.

Panic gripped the group as they realized the gravity of their situation. Sara's terrified cry echoed over the tumultuous sea as she clung to Matt, her arms wrapped tightly around him in a desperate attempt to shield him from the raging storm.

"We need to stay calm," John called out, his voice barely audible above the crashing waves. "We'll figure this out together."

But as the storm raged on, their hopes of survival dwindled with each passing moment. The waves grew larger and more ferocious, threatening to engulf the small boat in their frothy embrace.

John's heart pounded in his chest as he frantically scanned the horizon for any sign of land or rescue. But all he could see was an endless expanse of churning water and darkening skies, the storm showing no mercy to their plight.

The boat rocked violently as towering waves crashed against its sides, the wood groaning and creaking under the immense pressure. With a deafening crack, a rogue wave slammed into the boat's hull, splintering the wood into deadly shards. Suddenly, a sharp pain seared through John's leg, causing him to cry out in agony. He looked down to see a broken shard of wood protruding from his calf, blood seeping from the wound in a crimson stream.

Despite the excruciating pain, John's thoughts turned to Sara and Matt. With a surge of determination, he forced himself to his feet, his vision swimming with dizziness and pain. "Sara, Matt, take my life jacket!" he shouted, his voice hoarse with pain. "You need it more than I do. I'll be fine." But Sara shook her head, her eyes wide with fear. "No, John, we can't leave you like this. We'll find another way."

Before John could protest, the boat lurched violently to one side, sending them all tumbling into the icy embrace of the sea. The world spun around him in a dizzying whirlwind of chaos and confusion as the storm consumed them completely.

And then, darkness descended, wrapping John in its cold embrace as he slipped into unconsciousness, the last thing he remembered the anguished cries of his family echoing over the roar of the storm.

## WHAT CAME AFTER THE STORM?

As I drifted in and out of consciousness, buffeted by the raging waves, fragments of memories flooded my mind like shards of shattered glass. In those fleeting moments of clarity, I was transported back to a time when life was simpler, when happiness was as abundant as the sea air that now stung my lungs.

I saw Sara's smile, radiant and warm, as she laughed with Matt in the soft glow of the setting sun. Their joy was infectious, filling my heart with a sense of contentment I had never known before.

I remembered the sound of Matt's laughter, the way it echoed across the harbor like a melody of pure joy. He was my light, my reason for being. In his laughter, I found solace amidst the chaos of the world.

And then there was Sara, my rock, my anchor in the stormy seas of life. Her unwavering love and support had been my guiding light, leading me through the darkest of days with grace and strength.

As the tumultuous waves tossed me to and fro, a memory emerged from the depths of my consciousness—a memory of the day I first laid eyes on Sara, a memory etched into the very fabric of my being.

I saw her standing there, a vision of grace and beauty, her eyes sparkling with warmth and intelligence as she greeted me with a smile that lit up the room. It was as if time stood still in that moment, the hustle and bustle of the world fading into the background as our gazes locked in a silent exchange of understanding.

There was an instant connection between us, a spark of recognition that ignited something deep within my soul. It was as if we had known each other for a lifetime, our hearts beating in sync as if guided by some unseen force of destiny.

We talked for hours that day, our conversation flowing effortlessly as if we had known each other for years. There was a chemistry between us that was undeniable, a magnetic pull drawing us closer with each passing moment.

Together, we had weathered the storms of life, standing side by side against the turbulent tide of fate. Our love was a beacon of hope in a world shrouded in darkness, a testament to the power of human connection.

But now, as the waves tossed me like a ragdoll upon the merciless sea, those memories felt like distant echoes in the vast expanse of my mind. The pain in my leg throbbed with every heartbeat, a cruel reminder of the fragility of life.

## SURVIVAL

I awoke to the sound of crashing waves and the sensation of rough sand against my skin. My head throbbed with a dull ache, and my body felt heavy and sluggish, as if I were trapped in some kind of waking nightmare. Slowly, painfully, I became aware of a presence beside me—a shadowy figure kneeling in the sand, their hands gripping my shoulders with a strength born of desperation. Through the haze of pain and confusion, I could feel them tugging me away from the sea and towards the safety of the land.

I drifted in and out of consciousness, the world around me a blur of muted colors and indistinct shapes. At times, I felt as though I were drowning in the darkness, the weight of exhaustion dragging me deeper into its depths. But then, like a beacon in the night, a flicker of awareness would pull me back to the surface, if only for a fleeting moment. Finally, mercifully, I awoke to find myself lying on the shore, the chilling night air kissing my skin with gentle caresses. Blinking against the darkness, I struggled to orient myself, my senses dulled by the residual effects of the deadly storm that brought me to this place. And then I saw him—Jake, his silhouette illuminated by the flickering glow of a small fire.

"Jake," I croaked, my voice hoarse with thirst and exhaustion. "What... what happened?"

Jake turned towards me, his expression a mixture of concern and relief. "You're awake," he said, his voice rough with emotion. "You've been out for a day. I found you washed up on the shore." I struggled to sit up, my muscles protesting with every movement. As I surveyed my surroundings, the reality of our situation began to sink in—the desolate beach, the distant sound of crashing waves, the overwhelming sense of isolation that hung heavy in the air.

As the haze of unconsciousness lifted, memories flooded back, each one a painful echo of the storm's wrath. The stark reality hit me like a physical blow—Matt and Sarah were not here. Panic surged within me, a wild torrent of fear and dread. "Matt! Sarah!" I called out frantically, my voice ragged with desperation. "Where are they?" Jake, with a somber expression, met my distressed gaze. "I searched everywhere," he began, his voice heavy with sorrowful truth. "There's no sign of them." Shock and disbelief held me momentarily captive, but urgency soon propelled me into action. Ignoring the searing pain in my leg, I attempted to rise, my muscles straining against the agony and the weight of uncertainty. "Help me up," I demanded, a mixture of fear and determination in my eyes.

Jake hesitated, concern etched deeply on his face. "John, your leg—" "I don't care," I interrupted, my voice strained with urgency. "We have to find them." With Jake's steady support, I managed to rise, albeit with agonizing effort. Every movement sent bolts of pain shooting through my injured leg, a relentless reminder of our dire situation. Ignoring the protests of my body, I scanned the shoreline, hoping against hope for a glimpse of Matt and Sarah, praying for some sign of their presence. "They can't be far," I muttered more to myself than to Jake, a mantra of hope amidst the chaos of despair. But the relentless sea offered no answers, its vast expanse swallowing any trace of our missing companions. Exhausted and defeated, I sank back onto the sand, frustration and anguish warring within me. "We have to keep looking," I insisted, my voice hollow with unspoken fears.

Jake's eyes darkened with concern as he knelt beside me, his hands gentle as he inspected the makeshift splint. "You broke it when we washed up on the shore," he explained, his voice tinged with regret. "I did what I could to set it, but... it's bad, John. Real bad." I swallowed hard, the reality of our predicament settling over me like a suffocating shroud. We were stranded on a deserted island, with no hope of rescue and no guarantee of survival. And yet, even in the face of such overwhelming odds, I knew that as long as Jake and I stood together, there was still a chance—a chance to weather the storm, defy the odds, and emerge from this ordeal stronger and more resilient than ever before. With a deep breath, I pushed aside the pain and the fear, focusing instead on the flickering flame of the fire and the steady rhythm of the waves.

Jake placed a comforting hand on my shoulder, his touch a reassuring anchor amidst the chaos of our circumstances. "I'll go back out and search again," he promised, determination firming his features. "But we need to be cautious. The storm may have scattered them or worse..."

His unspoken words hung heavy in the air, each possibility more ominous than the last. I nodded, swallowing the bitter taste of fear that threatened to overwhelm me. "Just... hurry," I managed, my voice strained with unspoken worry.

As Jake ventured back into the rugged terrain, my thoughts raced, alternating between memories of the storm's fury and the grim reality of our present situation. The pain in my leg, a constant reminder of our ordeal, pulsed with every heartbeat, a cruel rhythm to accompany my anxious thoughts.

When Jake returned, his expression somber, my heart sank. "No sign of them," he reported, his voice barely above a whisper. "We'll keep searching, but for now, we need to focus on survival."

I couldn't shake the gnawing ache in my chest, the weight of grief pressing down on me like a suffocating blanket. Sara and Matt—my beloved wife and son—were out there somewhere, lost to the merciless embrace of the sea. The mere thought of their absence was enough to send waves of anguish crashing over me, threatening to pull me under.

"John," Jake's voice cut through the silence like a lifeline, his eyes filled with empathy and understanding. "I know… I know it's hard. But we have to stay strong. For them." His words were like a balm to my wounded soul, offering a sliver of solace amidst the storm of emotions raging within me. But even as I nodded in silent agreement, the tears welled up in my eyes, threatening to spill over at any moment. "They were everything to me, Jake," I whispered, my voice choked with emotion. "I can't… I can't bear the thought of never seeing them again." Jake reached out a hand, his touch a comforting presence against my trembling shoulder. "I know, John. I know," he murmured softly. "But we can't lose hope. We have to believe that they're out there, somewhere, waiting for us to find them."

As Jake's words sank in, a torrent of emotions threatened to engulf me. The uncertainty, the fear, the relentless ache for my son and wife—I couldn't contain it any longer. Tears welled up, blurring my vision as I struggled to hold back sobs that clawed their way up my throat. "Go! We have to find them," I pleaded, my voice cracking with desperation and grief. "They can't be gone, Jake. They can't." Every fiber of my being rebelled against the thought of losing them, against the idea of a future without Sara's warmth, without Matt's laughter echoing through our lives. The weight of helplessness bore down on me, a crushing burden that threatened to suffocate hope itself.

But Jake, with a patience born of shared sorrow, placed a hand on my shoulder, his touch a silent anchor in the storm raging within me. "We will, John," he said softly, his voice a whisper of determination against the howling winds of despair. "We'll search every inch of this shore tomorrow until we find them."

~

As the first rays of dawn painted the sky with hues of pink and gold, Jake rose from his makeshift bed, his footsteps soft against the sand as he made his way towards the dense foliage that bordered the far side of the island. Jake was preparing to venture into the unknown depths of the island, and I couldn't help but feel a twinge of anxiety gnawing at the pit of my stomach. "Hey, Jake," I called out, my voice hesitant. "Be careful out there, alright?"

Jake turned towards me, a reassuring smile playing at the corners of his lips. "Don't worry, John," he said, his tone confident. "I'll be fine. I'll just have a look around, see if I can find us something to eat." I nodded, though the worry still lingered in the back of my mind. "Just... be cautious," I urged, my voice tinged with concern. "We don't know what's out there." Jake clapped a hand on my shoulder, his touch grounding me in the midst of my swirling emotions. "I'll keep my wits about me, don't you worry," he reassured me, his gaze steady. "You just focus on resting up and taking care of yourself, alright?"

With a reluctant nod, I watched as Jake disappeared into the foliage, his figure gradually fading from view until he was nothing more than a distant speck against the lush greenery of the island. Left alone with my thoughts once more, I settled back against the sand, the rhythmic crash of the waves providing a soothing backdrop to the tumult of emotions swirling within me. As I waited for Jake's return, I couldn't help but wonder what he would find out there amidst the tangled undergrowth of the island. Would he discover a hidden trove of edible fruits and berries, or perhaps stumble upon a freshwater spring to quench our thirst? The possibilities were endless, and yet so too were the dangers lurking in the shadows, waiting to ensnare the unwary traveler in their deadly embrace. Left alone with my thoughts, I watched him go, a pang of loneliness echoing in the depths of my soul. But instead of focusing on the present, my mind drifted back to a time when the sea had been a place of joy and laughter—a time when Sara and I had stood on the shore, our hearts intertwined like the crashing waves that danced at our feet.

I could almost feel the warmth of the sun on my skin, the salty breeze tousling my hair as I held Sara's hand in mine, our fingers intertwined in a silent promise of forever. The sea stretched out before us, a boundless expanse of possibility, its rhythmic cadence a soothing melody to our troubled souls. Sara's laughter echoed in my ears, pure and joyous as she danced along the water's edge, her laughter mingling with the cries of seagulls soaring overhead. In that moment, with the sea as our witness, we were free—free from the burdens of the past, free from the uncertainties of the future, free to simply be. And then, as if summoned by the gentle tug of memory, Sara turned towards me, her eyes sparkling with love and affection. "John," she whispered, her voice a soft caress against the wind. "I love you." I wrapped my arms around her, pulling her close as if to shield her from the harsh realities of the world. "I love you too, Sara," I murmured, my voice barely audible above the sound of the waves. "More than words could ever express."

In that fragile state between wakefulness and dreams, where reality blurs with imagination, I saw him—Matt, my little boy, darting along the shoreline with infectious laughter. It was a brief flicker, a mirage of joy that momentarily lifted the heavy burden of grief from my heart. "Matt!" I called out, my voice catching with emotion as I stumbled forward, hoping against hope that somehow, by some miracle, he was there. His face turned towards me, his grin as bright as a sunbeam, and my heart soared with a mixture of elation and disbelief.

"Dad!" His voice carried on the breeze, a melody of love and innocence that I had yearned to hear once more. He beckoned me with outstretched arms, and I moved towards him, fueled by a father's boundless love and an unspoken wish to hold him close again. But with each step, reality crept back in, blurring the edges of his form, softening his laughter into distant echoes. The truth hung heavy in the air—a bittersweet reminder that what I sought was but a memory, a whisper of what once was. Tears welled in my eyes as I stood there, the crash of waves a symphony of grief that matched the storm within. "I'm sorry, Dad," the fading echoes seemed to say, carrying with them the weight of unspoken conversations and cherished moments.

But then, like light cutting through the fog, a gentle nudge brought me back to the present, the warmth of Jake's touch grounding me in the here and now. Blinking against the haze of confusion, I opened my eyes to find him kneeling beside me, his expression a mixture of concern and relief. "John, you're awake," Jake's voice was a welcome sound in the silence, his eyes soft with relief as he helped me sit up. "I was starting to worry." I offered him a weak smile, the remnants of my hallucination still lingering in the corners of my mind. "I'm okay, Jake," I assured him, though the words felt hollow on my lips. "Just... just a bad dream, I think."

Jake nodded in understanding, his gaze lingering on me for a moment longer before he turned his attention to the bundle he carried in his arms. With a sense of anticipation, he unwrapped the makeshift package to reveal a bounty of meat—freshly caught and ready to be cooked. "There were Terns on the other side of the island," Jake explained, his eyes alight with excitement. "I managed to catch a few. It's not much, but it's something." Confusion flickered across my face, prompting Jake to elaborate, "Terns are seabirds, quite agile flyers. Their meat isn't abundant, but it's nourishing." I couldn't help but feel a surge of gratitude towards Jake, his resourcefulness providing us with a much-needed source of sustenance in our time of need.

With a renewed sense of purpose, I watched as he set about preparing the meat, his hands deft and sure as he fashioned a makeshift grill from the debris scattered around our camp. Meanwhile, I gathered dry twigs and leaves to start a fire. It took a few tries, but soon we had a crackling fire going. Once the flames settled into a steady glow, Jake skewered the Tern meat pieces on thin branches and placed them over the fire. We watched as the meat began to sizzle and cook, the savory smell making our stomachs growl in anticipation. Jake turned the skewers occasionally, making sure each side cooked evenly.

And then, finally, the moment of truth arrived—Jake carefully removed the cooked meat from the makeshift grill, its golden-brown exterior glistening in the flickering light of the fire. With trembling hands, he handed me a portion, his eyes alight with anticipation as we shared a silent moment of gratitude. As Jake handed me a portion of the cooked meat, my stomach lurched with hunger, a primal instinct kicking in as the savory aroma wafted through the air. Without a second thought, I dug in, my hands trembling with anticipation as I tore into the tender flesh like a starving animal. Beside me, Jake mirrored my actions, his movements just as frantic and desperate as my own. There was no elegance in the way we ate, no manners or decorum as we devoured the meat with a raw intensity that bordered on desperation. Juice dripped down my chin, staining my shirt as I tore off another mouthful, barely pausing to chew before swallowing it whole.

Once we were done eating. I looked over to Jake."I need you to search for Matt and Sarah," I said firmly. "Head south along the shoreline. I'll stay here and keep the fire going."

Jake nodded, understanding the urgency in my voice. He helped me settle comfortably by the tent, making sure that my injured leg was propped up on a makeshift cushion. "I'll be back soon," Jake reassured, his eyes reflecting both concern and determination.

It was only a while that was spent when Jake was gone and I couldn't bear sitting here, not being able to look for my wife and son myself. Ignoring the dull ache that throbbed in my leg, I pushed myself upright, my muscles protesting as I tested my weight on unsteady legs. With each step, the pain flared anew, but I pressed on, driven by a desperate need to escape the suffocating confines of our camp. The sun beat down mercilessly as I stumbled forward, my breath coming in ragged gasps as I trudged through the sand. The island stretched out before me, a barren wasteland devoid of life or hope—a stark reminder of the desolation that had become our reality. And then, as if by some cruel twist of fate, I stumbled upon it—a small blue jacket buried in the sand, half-buried beneath a mound of debris. My heart lurched in my chest as I reached out to touch it, my fingers trembling as they brushed against the familiar fabric. And then it hit me—a wave of raw, unbridled emotion that threatened to consume me whole. With a cry of anguish, I fell to my knees, tears streaming down my cheeks as I clutched the jacket to my chest, my cries echoing across the empty expanse of the island.

"Why?" I screamed, my voice raw with pain and despair. "Why did this happen to us? What did we do to deserve this?"

And so, I raged against the injustice of it all, my cries of anguish echoing into the void as I cursed the cruel hand of fate that had torn my family apart. And then, as if in response to my cries, Jake came running, his face covered with concern as he knelt beside me, his arms wrapping around me in a gesture of comfort. "John, it's okay," he murmured, his voice a soothing balm against the storm of emotion raging within me. "We'll get through this together. I promise." But his words were lost on me, drowned out by the overwhelming tide of grief that threatened to consume me whole. With a final sob, I succumbed to the darkness that beckoned, my consciousness slipping away as Jake carried me back to the safety of our shelter, his arms a lifeline in the tumultuous sea of despair.

By the third day on the island, Jake's face wore a somber expression as he returned from his hunt for food. His footsteps, once filled with purpose and determination, now seemed heavy with disappointment. "John," he said, his voice tinged with resignation as he sank down beside me by the fire. "I'm afraid there are no more Terns on the island. They've migrated, and there's nothing left for us to catch." His words hung in the air like a heavy cloud, casting a pall over our already bleak situation. I felt a sinking sensation in the pit of my stomach as the reality of our predicament sank in—without a source of food, our chances of survival grew even slimmer.

I tried to swallow past the lump in my throat, my mind racing as I searched for a solution to our dilemma. But try as I might, I couldn't shake the feeling of despair that threatened to overwhelm me. "We'll figure something out, Jake," I said, though the words sounded hollow even to my own ears. "We've come this far, haven't we? We'll find a way to make it through." But deep down, I knew that the odds were stacked against us. With each passing day, our situation grew more dire, our chances of rescue slipping further and further away.

# HALLUCINATIONS & THE RESCUE

I found myself transported back to a time when life was simple and carefree. In my mind's eye, Sara stood at the helm of our boat, her laughter mingling with the gentle lapping of waves against the hull. Matt, his face flushed with excitement, sat beside me, his small hands clutching a fishing rod as he eagerly awaited his first catch. And beside me, Jake, his easy smile a testament to the camaraderie we shared as we set out on yet another fishing trip.

But as quickly as the illusion had come, it shattered, leaving me gasping for breath as the harsh reality of our situation came crashing back down upon me. There was no boat, no laughter, no sense of normalcy—only the desolate expanse of the island stretching out before me, a grim reminder of the harsh truth we faced. With a heavy sigh, I pushed myself upright, the hunger gnawing at my insides serving as a cruel reminder of the perilous situation we found ourselves in. Reality hit hard—there were no Terns left on the island, and our chances of finding food grew slimmer by the day.

As the days dragged on, a heavy cloud of despair settled over us like a suffocating blanket, weighing down our spirits and dimming the spark of hope that had once burned bright within us. Hunger gnawed at our stomachs, relentless and unforgiving, while the relentless sun beat down upon us, sapping our strength and leaving us drained. Conversations between Jake and me grew sparse, our words falling flat in the oppressive silence that surrounded us. Where once there had been laughter and camaraderie, now there was only the hollow echo of our own voices, a stark reminder of the emptiness that had settled in our hearts. Our movements became sluggish, our actions guided more by instinct than conscious thought. We stumbled through the days in a daze, our minds clouded by hunger and fatigue, our bodies worn down by the relentless grind of survival.

And then there were the hallucinations—tricks of the mind that danced on the edges of our consciousness, taunting us with visions of a reality that was no longer attainable. Sara's laughter seemed to linger in the air, while Matt's voice echoed in the distance—a cruel reminder of all that we had lost. We tried to push the visions aside, to focus on the task at hand, but they lingered like ghosts, haunting us at every turn. It became harder and harder to distinguish between what was real and what was merely a figment of our fevered imaginations. Despite our best efforts, the hunger and despair gnawed at us, eroding our resolve and sapping our strength. There were moments when it felt as though we were teetering on the edge of madness, our grip on reality slipping further and further away with each passing day.

As Jake and I sat on the shore, our eyes scanning the horizon for any sign of hope, a glimmer of movement caught our attention—a small boat bobbing on the waves in the distance, its silhouette barely visible against the backdrop of the open sea. For a moment, we sat frozen in disbelief, the realization slowly dawning upon us that salvation was within reach. With a surge of adrenaline, Jake leapt to his feet, his movements quick and decisive as he raced to gather tinder for a fire.

"John, help me gather some dry wood," he called out, his voice tinged with urgency. "We need to light a signal fire to let them know we're here." I scrambled to my feet, my heart pounding in my chest as I joined Jake in gathering fuel for the fire. Together, we piled the wood high, the crackling flames casting long shadows across the sand as we worked to ignite the tinder. As the fire roared to life, sending plumes of smoke spiraling into the sky, I felt a surge of hope wash over me—a flicker of optimism amidst the despair that had threatened to consume us whole. We watched with bated breath as the boat drew nearer, its sleek form cutting through the waves with purpose and determination. And then, with a sense of relief that bordered on disbelief, we saw them—a group of rescuers, their faces alight with the glow of the fire as they steered the boat towards the shore. As they drew closer, I felt a lump form in my throat—a mixture of gratitude and disbelief swelling within me as I realized that we were finally being saved. With shaky hands, I waved frantically, my voice hoarse with emotion as I called out to them, my words lost amidst the roar of the surf.

But they saw us, their eyes locking onto our figures on the shore as they guided the boat towards us with practiced precision. And then, with a soft thud, the boat came to rest on the sand, its hull scraping against the shore as the rescuers leapt onto the beach, their faces etched with concern. "Are you okay?" one of them asked, his voice filled with compassion as he helped us to our feet. "We saw your signal fire and came as quickly as we could." Tears filled my eyes as I nodded, overcome with relief at the sight of our rescuers. Jake clapped a hand on my shoulder, his own eyes shining with gratitude as he thanked the strangers who had come to our aid. Together, we climbed aboard the boat, our hearts soaring with the knowledge that we were finally safe. As the rescuers guided us away from the island, I cast one final glance over my shoulder, bidding farewell to the desolate landscape that had been our home for so long.

As the boat carried us away from the island, a flood of emotions washed over me, threatening to drown me in a sea of grief and despair. I couldn't help but think back to the day when Sara and Matt had been by my side, their laughter mingling with the sound of the waves as we embarked on our journey across the same sea. And now, as I stood on the deck of the boat,

I was returning home alone—a hollow shell of the man I had once been. Memories of our past life together haunted me, each one a painful reminder of all that I had lost. I could still see Sara's smile, feel the warmth of her touch, hear Matt's laughter ringing in my ears. They were with me, yet so far away, their absence a gaping wound that refused to heal. As we sailed further and further away from the island, a sense of finality settled over me—a quiet acceptance of the harsh reality that awaited me on the shore. The life that lay ahead seemed daunting and unfamiliar, a stark contrast to the comfort and familiarity of the life I had known with Sara and Matt by my side.

Amidst the whirlwind of thoughts and feelings raging inside me, one emotion stood out—the crushing weight of loss that threatened to drown me in its depths. It was a pain so intense, so consuming, that it felt like a physical ache, gnawing at my insides and leaving me gasping for breath. As the boat continued its journey towards the shore, I found myself engulfed in a storm of grief, unable to escape the overwhelming tide of emotions crashing over me. I surrendered myself to the torrent, letting the tears flow freely as I grappled with the enormity of my loss.

But amidst the pain, there was a glimmer of something else—a bittersweet reminder of the love that Sara and Matt had brought into my life. Their absence was a void that could never be filled, but their memory lived on in my heart, a beacon of light in the darkness that surrounded me.

## THE RETURN

As I slowly emerged from the haze of unconsciousness, the sterile white lights of the hospital room assaulted my senses, replacing the endless expanse of sea that had become my constant companion on the island. Blinking against the harsh glare, I struggled to make sense of my surroundings, my mind still clouded by the remnants of sleep. Beside me, Jake sat slumped in a chair, his rhythmic snores filling the room with a dull hum. His presence brought a strange sense of comfort, a reminder that I was no longer alone in this unfamiliar world of white walls and beeping machines. But as my gaze drifted down to my legs, a wave of panic washed over me, threatening to pull me under. One of my legs was gone, replaced by a mass of bandages and gauze—a grim reminder of the price I had paid for survival.

"Jake," I croaked, my voice hoarse with fear. "What happened?" Jake stirred, his eyes fluttering open as he registered my distress. "Hey, John," he murmured, his voice thick with sleep. "You're awake." But I wasn't satisfied with his vague answer. "My leg," I insisted, my heart pounding in my chest. "What happened to my leg?" Jake's expression softened, and he reached out to grasp my hand in his. "John, listen to me," he said gently. "Your leg was infected—badly. We had no choice but to amputate it to save your life."

The words hit me like a sledgehammer, each syllable driving home the brutal reality of my situation. My heart pounded in my chest, a wild, frantic rhythm that threatened to burst free from its confines. Panic surged through my veins, a tidal wave of fear and despair threatening to engulf me whole. "How could this be happening?" I whispered, my voice hoarse with disbelief. "How could I have lost a part of myself so suddenly and irrevocably?" Tears stung my eyes as the enormity of my loss washed over me, leaving me gasping for breath. I clutched at the sheets, my fingers trembling with the weight of my anguish. But amidst the chaos of my emotions, Jake's calming presence offered a glimmer of hope—a lifeline in the midst of my turmoil. His steady voice broke through the haze of my panic, anchoring me to the present moment. "It's going to be okay, John," he said, his words a soothing balm against the raw edges of my despair. "You're alive, and that's what matters."

But his reassurance fell on deaf ears as hysteria threatened to consume me whole. I thrashed against the sheets, my chest heaving with each ragged breath. The room spun around me, a blur of white walls and sterile instruments. "Please," I begged, my voice rising to a desperate plea. "Make it stop. Make the pain stop." Jake moved to my side, his touch gentle yet firm as he tried to calm the storm raging within me. But I pushed him away, my hands shaking with the force of my panic. "It hurts," I sobbed, the words torn from the depths of my soul. "It hurts so much." And then, like a beacon in the darkness, a nurse appeared at my bedside, her presence a soothing balm against the storm. She spoke to me in hushed tones, her voice a gentle melody that cut through the chaos of my mind. "Shh, it's okay," she murmured, her words a soothing whisper against the tumult of my thoughts. "You're safe now. We're here to help you."

The next morning, I awoke to find a sense of calm settling over me like a blanket, soothing the raw edges of my emotions. The storm of despair that had raged within me had ebbed away, leaving behind a quiet sense of acceptance. Eventually, the doctors deemed me fit to leave the hospital, and I found myself back in the familiar confines of my home. As I sat in the wheelchair, Jake guided me towards the car parked just outside the hospital entrance. The morning air was crisp, tinged with the scent of freshly cut grass and the distant hum of traffic. Jake's movements were steady and deliberate, his face set in a mask of solemn determination.

The car ride was a somber affair, the weight of our shared grief hanging heavy in the air like a suffocating blanket. The silence between us was palpable, punctuated only by the soft hum of the engine and the occasional sigh that escaped Jake's lips.

I watched the world pass by in a blur of colors and shapes, my thoughts consumed by the enormity of what lay ahead. The hospital, with its sterile hallways and fluorescent lights, felt like a distant memory—a mere blip on the radar of my existence. As we pulled up to my house, Jake helped me out of the car with a gentle hand, his touch a silent reassurance in the face of the unknown. The familiar sight of my home loomed before me, its windows dark and its doors closed tight against the outside world. I thanked Jake for his help, the words feeling hollow and empty in the silence that surrounded us. He nodded in response, his eyes betraying a hint of sadness that mirrored my own. "I'll come in with you," Jake offered, concern evident in his voice. I shook my head, my resolve firm despite the fatigue weighing down my limbs. "No, I need to do this alone. Thanks for everything." Jake hesitated, his expression torn between duty and concern. "Are you sure?" "Leave me, Jake," I said more forcefully, the urgency breaking through my exhaustion. Reluctantly, Jake nodded, his footsteps echoing away as he returned to his car, leaving me to face the emptiness that loomed within my own walls.

As I stepped over the threshold of my home, a tidal wave of emotions crashed over me, threatening to pull me under. The sound of the door closing behind me echoed through the silent halls, a solitary reminder of the emptiness that awaited me within. The familiar sights and sounds that greeted me—the cozy warmth of the living room, the faint scent of Sara's perfume lingering in the air, the echoes of Matt's laughter that seemed to reverberate off the walls—were like a cruel reminder of all that I had lost. Every corner of the house held memories of Sara and Matt, their presence etched into the very fabric of our home. The photographs that adorned the walls, capturing moments frozen in time; the toys scattered across the floor, waiting patiently for hands that would never play with them again; the empty spaces where their laughter once filled the air, now silent and still—it was as if they had never left, as if they were just beyond reach, waiting for me to call out to them.

But as I moved through the rooms, the reality of their absence pressed down upon me like a weight too heavy to bear. The emptiness that filled the spaces they had once occupied seemed to suffocate me, leaving me gasping for air in a sea of sorrow. I found myself drawn to the places where their presence lingered most—the kitchen, where Sara had prepared countless meals with love and care; the living room, where Matt had played with his toys for hours on end, his laughter ringing out like music; the bedroom, where we had shared whispered secrets in the darkness of the night, our love a beacon in the night. Each room held a piece of my heart, a fragment of the life we had once shared together. And yet, despite the familiarity of it all, there was an emptiness that pervaded every inch of the house—a hollow ache that threatened to consume me whole.

The weight of my grief crashing down upon me like a relentless wave. Tears streamed down my cheeks unchecked, my sobs echoing in the empty silence of the house. I longed to reach out and touch them, to feel their presence beside me once more, but they were gone—lost to me forever, their absence a gaping wound that refused to heal. And so I sat there, lost in a sea of memories and regrets, longing for a past that could never be reclaimed. The house that had once been a sanctuary now felt like a prison, its walls closing in around me, suffocating me with their silent reproach.

As the darkness descended upon the house like a heavy shroud, evenings brought little relief from the crushing weight of my grief. It was during one of these long, lonely nights that Jake came knocking at my door, his presence a welcome break from the suffocating silence that had enveloped me. I let him in with a heavy heart, my movements slow and deliberate as if weighed down by the burden of my sorrow.

"Hey, John," he greeted me, his voice filled with warmth and concern. "I thought I'd come by and see how you're holding up. It's been tough, huh?" I offered him a weak smile in return, though it felt more like a grimace than anything else. "Yeah, it has," I admitted, my voice barely above a whisper. "But I'm managing, I guess." We fell into a stilted conversation, the words flowing awkwardly between us like water trickling through a dry riverbed. Jake tried his best to lift my spirits, regaling me with stories of his own misadventures and offering words of encouragement, but it was all I could do to muster a half-hearted nod in response. As the night wore on, the conversation turned to more serious matters, and I found myself opening up to Jake in a way I hadn't before. I spoke of my longing to find closure, to lay Sara and Matt to rest once and for all.

"Jake," I began, my voice barely above a whisper, "I've been thinking... about Sara and Matt." Jake nodded solemnly, his expression mirroring my own as he reached out to place a comforting hand on my shoulder. "I know, John," he replied softly. "I miss them too." Tears welled up in my eyes at the mention of their names, the pain of their loss still fresh and raw despite the passing of time. "I can't shake this feeling, Jake," I confessed, my voice trembling with emotion. "I keep thinking...what if they're still out there?" Jake's brow furrowed in concern as he listened to my words, his eyes filled with empathy. "What do you mean, John?" he asked gently.

I took a deep breath, steeling myself for what I was about to say. "I mean... what if their bodies are still on the island?" I said, the words tumbling out in a rush. "What if we never found them?" The idea hung in the air between us, heavy and laden with unspoken dread. Jake's expression softened as he reached out to take my hand in his own, offering me a silent gesture of solidarity. "I understand, John," he said quietly. "But I searched that island from top to bottom. There's no way they could have survived out there for so long."

"How can you give up on them so quickly?" My voice cracked with emotion, the words echoing in the heavy silence between them. Jake's expression tightened slightly, his gaze steady but tinged with a flicker of discomfort. "It's not about giving up, John," he replied evenly, trying to maintain a sense of calm despite the rising tension. "I'm just trying to be realistic." "Realistic?" my voice rose. "Realistic would be exhausting every possible avenue to find them! They're out there, Jake. I know it." "I know you're hurting, John," Jake interjected, his voice gentle but firm. "We all are. But we have to face the facts. We've done everything we can." "I haven't done everything! I won't give up on them, Jake. I can't." For a moment, neither spoke, the silence filled only by the distant murmur of the waves against the shore. Finally, Jake spoke, his voice softer now, tinged with a touch of sadness. "John, I'm not asking you to give up. I'm asking you to consider what's best for everyone. We'll talk to the police, we'll do everything we can. But we also have to take care of ourselves."

"I'm tired, Jake," I admitted, exhaustion seeping into every word. "I think you should leave for now. I'll talk to you tomorrow." My voice carried a weariness that matched the weight of my emotions, a heavy burden pressing down on my shoulders.

Jake's expression softened with understanding, his features reflecting the shared fatigue between us. "Alright, John," he acquiesced, a hint of reluctance shadowing his gaze. "I'll check in on you tomorrow."

## STUCK IN THE PAST

The morning sun cast long shadows as I made my way to the local police station, my footsteps heavy with the weight of anticipation. With each step, my heart pounded in my chest, a nervous rhythm that matched the anxious thoughts racing through my mind. As I entered the station, the familiar scent of polished wood and stale coffee greeted me, a stark contrast to the tumultuous emotions churning within me. Taking a deep breath to steady my nerves, I approached the front desk, where a weary-looking officer glanced up from his paperwork.

"Can I help you?" he asked, his voice tinged with a hint of impatience.

Clearing my throat, I forced myself to meet his gaze. "I need to speak with someone about a missing persons case," I said, my voice wavering slightly with emotion. The officer raised an eyebrow, his expression shifting from annoyance to curiosity. "Do you have a name?" he inquired, reaching for a notepad and pen. Swallowing hard, I steadied myself before speaking. "My name is John Salter," I replied, the words heavy on my tongue. "And I'm here to report my wife and son as missing." As I spoke, I could feel the weight of the past pressing down on me, the memories of that fateful boat outing threatening to overwhelm me once more. But I pushed the thoughts aside, focusing instead on the task at hand. The officer listened intently as I recounted the events leading up to my family's disappearance, his brow furrowing with concern as I spoke. When I had finished, he nodded solemnly, his expression grave.

"I'm sorry to hear about your situation, Mr. Salter," he said, his voice tinged with sympathy. "We'll do everything we can to help." Relief flooded through me at his words, a flicker of hope igniting within me once more. "Thank you," I replied, gratitude coloring my tone.

With a few quick keystrokes, the officer summoned a colleague to join us, explaining the situation as we waited. Before long, a senior officer emerged from the back offices, his demeanor serious as he approached. "Mr. Salter, I'm Detective Reynolds," he said, extending a hand in greeting. "I understand you have a missing persons case you'd like to report." I nodded, my throat tightening with emotion. "Yes, Detective," I replied, struggling to keep my voice steady. "My wife, Sara, and our son, Matt, went missing during a boating trip three weeks ago. I need your help to find them."

Detective Reynolds listened attentively as I recounted the details of our ill-fated outing, his expression growing more serious with each passing moment. When I had finished, he nodded thoughtfully, his gaze flickering to the officers gathered around us. "We'll need to launch an investigation right away," he said, his tone decisive. "I'll have a team assembled and ready to go after some discussion with the authorities." As the plan to launch an investigation took shape, I couldn't shake the gnawing sense of urgency that consumed me. Every fiber of my being yearned to return to that forsaken island, to scour its shores for any trace of my wife and son. But as I voiced my desire to join the search party, Detective Reynolds gently shook his head, his expression tinged with concern.

"I appreciate your willingness to help, Mr. Salter," he said, his tone measured. "But we can't risk putting you in harm's way. We don't know what we might find on that island, and I can't guarantee your safety." His words struck me like a blow to the chest, the reality of my situation crashing down on me once more. Despite my desperate longing to find Sara and Matt, I knew deep down that he was right. The island held too many secrets, too many dangers lurking in its shadowed depths.

As Detective Reynolds and I continued our conversation, another figure emerged from the depths of the police station, his presence commanding attention as he approached. "Mr. Salter, I'm Detective Mike," he said, extending a hand in greeting. "I couldn't help but overhear your conversation with Detective Reynolds. Your story is…compelling, to say the least."

I nodded, my gaze flickering between the two detectives as they exchanged a meaningful glance. There was something about Detective Mike's demeanor that set him apart from his colleague, a sense of quiet intensity that hinted at a depth of experience beyond his years. "I've dealt with cases like this before," Detective Mike continued, his voice low and measured. "Cases where the truth is elusive, and the answers are buried beneath layers of deceit and deception. But I believe that with the right approach, we can uncover the truth behind your wife and son's disappearance."

I dialed Jake's number with trembling fingers, my heart pounding in my chest as I waited for him to answer. When his voice finally came through the line, I wasted no time in blurting out the news, my words tumbling over each other in my haste. "Jake, they're sending a search party to the island," I said, my voice tinged with urgency. "They're going to look for Sara and Matt, try to find out what happened to them." There was a brief pause on the other end of the line, the silence stretching between us like a chasm. When Jake finally spoke, his voice was laced with a hint of unease, a tremor of fear beneath the surface. "John, are you sure this is a good idea?" he asked, his words cautious. "What if…what if they don't find anything? What if…what if we're better off not knowing?" His words sent a chill down my spine, a wave of doubt crashing over me like a relentless tide. But even as I grappled with my own fears and uncertainties, I knew that I couldn't turn back now. The need for answers burned within me, a fire that refused to be extinguished. "I have to do this, Jake," I replied, my voice firm despite the tremor of doubt that lingered in my words. "I need to know what happened to them, no matter what."

~

As the call with John ended, Jake felt a heavy weight settle in his chest, his mind already whirring with plans and strategies. He knew what needed to be done, and he was the only one capable of doing it. With a sense of determination, Jake set about his task, his fingers flying across the keys of his phone as he dialed a number from memory. The phone rang once, twice, before a familiar voice answered on the other end. "Agent Reynolds," came the crisp greeting, the voice tinged with authority.

"It's me," Jake replied, his tone curt and businesslike. "I need a favor." There was a pause on the other end of the line, the silence pregnant with unspoken questions. But Jake wasted no time in getting to the point, laying out his request in clear and concise terms. "I need you to put a stop to the search party that's heading to the island," he said, his words leaving no room for argument. "I don't care what it takes, just make sure they don't find anything." There was a moment of hesitation before Agent Reynolds responded, his voice guarded. "I can't just shut down a police operation without cause," he said, his words carefully measured.

Jake's jaw clenched in frustration, his patience wearing thin. "I don't care about protocols or red tape," he snapped. "I need this done, and I need it done now." There was another pause on the line, the tension between them palpable. But finally, Agent Reynolds relented, his tone resigned. "Alright," he said, his voice heavy with reluctance. "I'll see what I can do."

With that, the call ended, leaving Jake to stew in his thoughts. He knew he was taking a risk by involving Agent Reynolds, but he was willing to do whatever it took to protect his secrets. And as he waited for the outcome of his request, Jake couldn't help but wonder what the future held in store. The minutes stretched into hours as Jake paced restlessly around his living room, his mind racing with a thousand different scenarios. He knew the stakes were high, but he was willing to do whatever it took to keep the truth buried. As the clock ticked relentlessly on, Jake's anxiety only grew, a knot of tension coiling in the pit of his stomach. Finally, the phone rang, shattering the suffocating silence that had settled over the room. With a quick glance at the caller ID, Jake's heart leaped into his throat as he answered the call.

"Agent Reynolds?" he asked, his voice strained with anticipation. "It's done," came the curt reply, the words sending a surge of relief coursing through Jake's veins. "The search party has been called off. There won't be any interference from law enforcement." A wave of gratitude washed over Jake as he thanked Agent Reynolds for his help, his mind already racing with plans for the next phase of his operation. With the search party out of the picture, he was one step closer to achieving his goal, one step closer to ensuring that his secrets remained hidden.

But even as he celebrated this small victory, Jake couldn't shake the feeling of unease that gnawed at the edges of his consciousness. He knew he was treading on dangerous ground, playing a dangerous game with forces beyond his control. And as he pondered the implications of his actions, a seed of doubt took root in his mind, whispering darkly of the consequences that awaited him if his secrets were ever revealed. But for now, Jake pushed aside his doubts and fears, focusing instead on the task at hand. With the search party out of the way, he was free to continue his mission unabated, to ensure that his secrets remained buried forever. And as he set about making the necessary preparations, Jake couldn't help but feel a sense of grim satisfaction, knowing that he was one step closer to achieving his goal. But little did he know that his actions had set in motion a chain of events that would ultimately lead to his downfall, that the truth he sought to bury would one day rise to the surface, tearing apart the fragile facade he had worked so hard to maintain.

~

The tension in the police station room was thick and suffocating as the agents delivered their devastating news. My heart pounded in my chest, the blood roaring in my ears like a raging tempest as their words sank in with a sickening finality. "We're sorry, Mr. Salter," one of the agents said, his voice laced with a heavy dose of regret. "But we can't proceed with the search party. It hasn't been authorized by the police or the higher authorities." The words hit me like a physical blow, knocking the wind from my lungs and leaving me reeling in disbelief. How could they just call off the search like that, leaving Sara and Matt's fate hanging in the balance? It was unfathomable, incomprehensible, and it filled me with a sense of righteous anger that burned like a white-hot flame in the pit of my stomach. I felt the fury bubbling up inside me, a primal rage that threatened to consume me whole. "What do you mean, you can't proceed?" I demanded, my voice rising to a fevered pitch. "You can't just abandon them out there! They're my wife and son, damn it!"

But the agents remained unmoved, their expressions stoic and impassive as they delivered their rehearsed lines with practiced detachment. "I'm sorry, Mr. Salter," one of them repeated, his tone devoid of emotion. "But without proper authorization, we can't proceed with the search." I felt my control slipping, the anger boiling over into a seething cauldron of rage. "You spineless cowards!" I shouted, my voice echoing off the walls of the room. "You're just going to leave them out there to rot? Is that it? Is that what you call justice?"

But my words fell on deaf ears, the agents maintaining their stony façade as if nothing I said could penetrate their carefully constructed defenses. I could feel the fury building inside me, a raging inferno that threatened to consume me whole. Without thinking, I lunged forward, my fists clenched in impotent rage as I advanced on the agents with murder in my eyes. "You're going to regret this," I snarled, my voice a guttural growl of fury. "I'll make you regret every single word you've said!" But before I could reach them, strong arms closed around my waist, pulling me back with a strength born of desperation. "John, stop!" a familiar voice cried out, the sound cutting through the haze of my rage like a knife through butter. It was Jake, his face pale and drawn as he struggled to restrain me from doing something foolish. "You need to calm down, man," he said, his voice strained with effort. "This isn't going to help anyone." But I was beyond reason, lost in a maelstrom of fury and despair. "They can't just abandon them!" I roared, my voice raw with emotion. "I won't let them get away with this!"

But Jake held fast, his grip unyielding as he fought to bring me back from the brink of madness. "You need to think this through, John," he said, his voice firm but gentle. "We can't let our emotions cloud our judgment. We need to find another way." But I was beyond reason, lost in a sea of anger and despair. "No!" I cried, my voice a desperate plea for justice. "I won't let them get away with this! I won't rest until I find them, until I bring them home!" But even as the words left my lips, I knew that my efforts were in vain. The agents remained unmoved, their resolve unshaken as they stood before me like cold, unfeeling sentinels of the law.

Jake's silent presence was a comfort as he drove me home, the rhythmic hum of the engine lulling me into a daze as the world outside passed by in a blur. The weight of the day's events pressed heavily upon me, the ache in my heart threatening to consume me whole. As we pulled up to my house, Jake turned to me with a sympathetic look in his eyes, his hand resting reassuringly on my shoulder. "Take care of yourself, John," he said softly. "I'll be here if you need anything." I nodded, offering him a weak smile as I stepped out of the car and made my way up the path to my front door. The familiar surroundings offered little solace as I stumbled inside, my footsteps heavy with exhaustion as I collapsed onto the sofa in the dimly lit living room.

The floodgates opened then, the tears flowing freely as the weight of my grief threatened to crush me under its weight. I sobbed uncontrollably, the pain of loss ripping through me like a knife as I struggled to come to terms with the reality of my shattered dreams. And then, as exhaustion finally claimed me, I drifted into a fitful sleep, the echoes of my sobs fading into the darkness as I slipped into the realm of dreams. In the dream, I found myself back on the boat, the warm embrace of the sun kissing my skin as I watched Sara and Matt play in the gentle waves. Their laughter filled the air, a symphony of joy that lifted my spirits and eased the ache in my heart. Matt's infectious giggles filled the air as he chased after Terns, his tiny hands reaching out to grab at the salty spray that danced on the wind. I couldn't help but smile as I watched them, the love I felt for my wife and son swelling in my chest until it threatened to burst. It was moments like these that made all the struggles and hardships of life worth it, moments of pure, unadulterated joy that I wished could last forever.

But as I basked in the warmth of our perfect moment, a shadow fell over us, casting a pall of darkness over our idyllic scene. I looked up, my heart sinking as I saw a dark cloud looming on the horizon, its edges tinged with a sickly shade of gray. A sense of unease crept over me, the hairs on the back of my neck standing on end as a chill ran down my spine. I glanced over at Sara, but her attention was focused on the task at hand, her brow furrowed in concentration as she prepared sandwiches for our impromptu picnic. And then, as if from out of nowhere, Jake appeared on deck, his features twisted into a mask of rage and madness. In his hand, he held a gun, its cold metal glinting ominously in the fading light. My heart lurched in my chest as I watched in horror, unable to move or speak as Jake took aim at Sara and Matt. Time seemed to slow to a crawl as I screamed out in silent terror, the sound lost in the void of the nightmare that surrounded me.

But no matter how hard I tried, I couldn't move, couldn't scream, couldn't do anything but watch helplessly as Jake pulled the trigger, the deafening roar of the gunshot shattering the fragile peace of our perfect moment. And then, with a sickening thud, Sara and Matt crumpled to the ground, their lifeless bodies lying motionless at Jake's feet. I wanted to cry out, to run to them, to do anything to stop the nightmare from unfolding before my eyes. But I was paralyzed, trapped in the prison of my own fear and despair. And then, just as suddenly as it had begun, the nightmare ended, leaving me gasping for breath as I jolted awake in my bed. My heart pounded in my chest, my body drenched in a cold sweat as I struggled to shake off the remnants of the dream that still clung to me like a shroud of darkness. It took me a moment to realize that I was experiencing sleep paralysis, a terrifying phenomenon that left me unable to move or speak as I lay there, trapped in the grip of my own terror.

# NEW BEGINNINGS

The ache in my phantom limb woke me, a familiar pang that mirrored the emptiness in my chest. Images of Sarah's smile and Matt's laughter danced behind my eyelids, a cruel reminder of what I'd lost. Every morning was a battle against grief, a tide threatening to pull me under. Getting out of bed was a war I fought every single day. Grunting, I wrestled my prosthetic leg onto the nightstand, the cold metal a harsh contrast to my clammy skin. Each step, aided by the unforgiving grip of my cane, felt deliberate, a testament to my refusal to drown in the pain. Shower, dress, coffee. The silence of the apartment pressed in on me like a suffocating blanket. I booked a cab for the office, a place that offered a flimsy shield against the storm raging inside. The day stretched before me, a monotonous blur of meetings, reports, emails. A dull ache throbbed behind my eyes with every passing hour.

After some deliberation, I remembered a coworker's recommendation to join a local grief support group, a place where people gathered to share their burdens and find solace in the midst of loss. With a sense of trepidation mingled with hope, I took an Uber to the meeting while coming back from work, unsure of what to expect but desperate for a glimmer of understanding in the darkness that surrounded me.

The room was dimly lit, the soft glow of candles casting flickering shadows on the faces of those gathered. I took a seat among them, feeling a sense of kinship in their shared sorrow. As the meeting began, each person took turns sharing their stories, their words a balm to my wounded soul. When it was my turn to speak, I hesitated for a moment, the weight of my grief threatening to choke the words in my throat. But with a deep breath, I began to speak, pouring out the pain and sorrow that had consumed me since Sara and Matt's disappearance. The words flowed freely, tumbling out in a rush of emotion as I spoke of the life we had shared, of the love that had sustained us through the darkest of times. And as I spoke, a sense of catharsis washed over me, a release from the burden of grief that had weighed me down for so long.

As the meeting drew to a close, I found myself lingering in the dimly lit room, my thoughts still swirling with the weight of grief that had brought me there. It was then that I noticed her—a young woman with dark hair and a quiet strength in her eyes, sitting alone in a corner of the room.

Approaching her tentatively, I introduced myself, drawn to the calm aura that seemed to surround her. She greeted me with a gentle smile, her voice soft as she shared her own story of loss. Her name was Lisa, and her parents taken from her in a tragic accident that had left her adrift in a sea of grief. As we talked, she shared with me some of the wisdom passed down to her by her ancestors, insights gleaned from a culture that had long grappled with the harsh realities of life and death. She spoke of the importance of honoring those we had lost, of keeping their memory alive through rituals and ceremonies that celebrated their lives.

After the meeting dispersed, I found myself drawn to Lisa again. There was a quiet strength beneath her sadness that resonated with me. With a determined breath, I walked over to her. "Hi Lisa," I said, offering a friendly smile. "That was a powerful introduction you gave."

We fell into a comfortable conversation, discussing the meeting and its implications. We talked about our jobs, our hobbies, and even the strange weather that day. It was a normal conversation, a connection that felt genuine and easy. As the conversation began to wind down, I glanced at the clock. "Wow, is it that late already?" I exclaimed. "Looks like everyone's gone. Do you have a ride home?" Lisa shook her head slightly. "Actually, no. I was planning to call a cab." "Well," I offered, "my car is right here. I wouldn't mind giving you a lift if you'd like."

As I drove Lisa home after the meeting, the weight of the night's conversation hung heavy in the air between us. The streetlights cast long shadows across the road, illuminating the quiet streets in a soft, hazy glow. The hum of the engine provided a steady background noise, filling the silence that stretched between us. After a few moments of tense silence, I cleared my throat, feeling the weight of my own words heavy on my tongue. "So, Lisa… you shared a bit about your story back there. Mind if I ask you more about it?"

Lisa turned to look at me, her gaze guarded but open. "Sure, John. What do you want to know?" I took a deep breath, gathering my thoughts before I spoke. "Well, you see…I lost my wife and son in a boating accident," I began, the memories flooding back with painful clarity. "We were out on the water for my son's birthday, just a simple outing. But then a storm hit, and…and everything went wrong. We ended up stranded on an island for weeks." Lisa's eyes widened in shock, her hand flying to her mouth in disbelief. "Oh, John, I'm so sorry. That sounds like an absolute nightmare. How did you…how did you cope?" I shrugged, a bitter laugh escaping me. "Honestly, I'm still trying to figure that out. It's been rough, to say the least."

Lisa nodded, her expression filled with sympathy as she processed my words. After a moment, she sighed, her voice soft as she began to speak. "Well, John…I lost my parents in a car accident a few years ago," she confessed, her tone tinged with sadness. "It was…it was the hardest thing I've ever had to go through." I listened intently, my heart aching for her as she shared her pain. "I can't even imagine," I murmured, my voice barely above a whisper. "Losing someone you love…it changes you, doesn't it?" Lisa nodded, a tear glistening in the corner of her eye. "Yeah, it does," she agreed softly. "But you know, John...it's okay to not be okay. And it's okay to lean on others for support when you need it."

I met her gaze, gratitude flooding through me for her understanding and compassion. "Thanks, Lisa," I said, my voice thick with emotion. "I really appreciate that." As we continued our journey through the quiet streets, the weight of our shared experiences hung heavy in the air. But in that moment, as we navigated through the darkness together, there was also a sense of solace and understanding—a glimmer of hope in the midst of our grief. We arrived at Lisa's house, and I helped her out of the car, the cool night air wrapping around us like a comforting embrace.

As I pulled into my driveway, I couldn't shake the feeling of emptiness that washed over me. The garage door grumbled shut behind me, the final, heavy sigh of the day. But the quiet outside wasn't a relief, it was a deafening roar in the emptiness of my house. Stepping inside, the scent of dust and loneliness hit me like a physical blow. Every corner held a ghost – Sarah's laugh echoing in the hallway, the imprint of Matt's tiny hand on the living room wall. My own footsteps felt alien on the familiar hardwood, a constant reminder of the two sets that were missing.

I moved on autopilot, putting away my things, the motions practiced from years of muscle memory. But the ache in my chest, the hollow where their love used to reside, gnawed at me with a fresh intensity. Sinking onto the couch, I buried my face in my hands, the dam finally breaking. Tears, hot and silent, streamed down my face. My chest constricted with each ragged breath, a sob escaping my lips before I could contain it. Images flickered behind my closed eyelids – a picnic in the park, Sarah's smile as bright as the sun, Matt's infectious giggle as he chased butterflies. The joy, the love, the life we once had – all so cruelly ripped away. The sounds of my grief echoed in the silent house, a raw and desperate plea for them to come back. But there was no answer, only the suffocating quiet that mirrored the emptiness inside me. Exhausted from weeping, I finally dragged myself to bed, the sheets cold against my clammy skin. Curled on my side, I clung to the faint scent of Sarah's perfume on a forgotten pillow, the last fragile tether to a life that was gone. Sleep, when it came, offered no solace, only a continuation of the relentless ache in my heart.

## HIDDEN GAMES

As I sat at my desk, the details of the Salter case swirling around in my mind, a sense of unease settled over me like a heavy fog. Something about the abrupt closure of the investigation didn't sit right with me, leaving a nagging feeling that there was more to the story than met the eye. Detective Reynolds' words echoed in my ears, his tone final and authoritative as he instructed us to drop the case. But I couldn't shake the feeling that there were unanswered questions, hidden truths waiting to be uncovered.

With a sense of determination burning within me, I resolved to dig deeper, to uncover the truth behind the Salter family's disappearance. I knew it wouldn't be easy, that there would be obstacles and resistance along the way. But I couldn't turn my back on the nagging sense of injustice that tugged at my conscience. As I delved into the case files spread out before me, I began to unravel a tangled web of deceit and corruption. There were whispers of powerful forces at play, pulling the strings from the shadows. There were too many inconsistencies, too many unanswered questions that begged for closer scrutiny.

One glaring omission stood out to me: Jake's testimony. It struck me as odd that Detective Reynolds had never taken his statement, never even called him in for questioning. It was as if Jake had slipped through the cracks, disappearing from the investigation without a trace.

But it was the mention of Terns that piqued my curiosity the most. According to John's account, he and Jake had survived on the island by hunting and eating Terns. However, my research revealed a startling truth: there were no Terns on the island where they were stranded. So what were they really hunting? As I sifted through the case files, another discrepancy caught my eye. Most of the wreckage from the island had washed up on the shore, yet there was no sign of Sara and Matt's bodies. It didn't make sense. How could everything else wash ashore, but not the bodies of the two missing family members?

I dialed Jake's number, the soft chime of the dial tone echoing in my ear as I waited for him to pick up. After a few rings, his voice crackled through the line, filled with a note of uncertainty. "Hey, Jake, it's Detective Mike calling from the precinct," I began, my tone casual but tinged with urgency. "I was hoping we could meet up for a chat. There are a few things I'd like to discuss with you." There was a moment of hesitation on the other end of the line, a palpable pause that stretched between us like a taut wire. I could sense Jake's reluctance, his apprehension evident in the hesitant cadence of his voice.

"Uh, sure, Mike," he replied, his words tinged with uncertainty. "I'm not sure what this is about, but...I guess I can meet you." I could hear the reluctance in his voice, the weight of unspoken questions lingering in the air between us. But I pushed aside my misgivings, focusing instead on the task at hand. "Great, how about we meet at the cafe on Main Street?" I suggested, my tone gentle but firm. "Say, around three o'clock?" There was a moment of silence as Jake considered my proposal, his hesitation evident in the drawn-out pause that followed.

"Okay, Mike," he finally replied, his tone resigned. "I'll see you there."

As I sat across from Jake in the cozy confines of the cafe, I couldn't shake the feeling of unease that gnawed at the edges of my consciousness. His casual demeanor belied the tension that simmered beneath the surface, a palpable undercurrent that threatened to engulf us both. I began our conversation with a casual inquiry about the storm, probing gently for details about their harrowing ordeal on the island. Jake's response was measured, his words tinged with a hint of apprehension as he recounted the events of that fateful day. But as he delved into the specifics of their survival, mentioning their reliance on Terns for sustenance, I felt a jolt of disbelief course through me.

"Wait a minute, Jake," I interjected, my voice cutting through the air like a knife. "Are you saying you survived on Terns?" My tone was casual, but beneath the surface, a torrent of questions raged within me. According to my research, there were no Terns native to the island during the time you were stranded there." Jake's reaction was immediate, a flicker of fear flashing across his features before he masked it with a practiced nonchalance. "Well, uh, yeah," he stammered, his voice faltering slightly. "I mean, there were other animals on the island too. We just…adapted to our surroundings, you know?" His words rang hollow in my ears, the truth obscured by a veil of uncertainty. Sensing my skepticism, Jake shifted uncomfortably in his seat, his eyes darting nervously around the room. It was clear that he was hiding something, a fact that only fueled my determination to uncover the truth.

As our conversation wore on, the atmosphere grew increasingly tense, the weight of unspoken truths hanging heavy between us. With each passing moment, I could feel the walls closing in around us, the facade of normalcy crumbling in the face of mounting suspicion. Finally, unable to bear the charade any longer, I brought our interrogation to an abrupt end, my words tinged with a note of finality. "Well, Jake, I appreciate your cooperation," I said, rising from my seat with a sense of resignation. "But I think we both know there's more to this story than meets the eye." Jake's response was a mere nod, his gaze averted as he muttered a perfunctory farewell. As I made my way out of the cafe, I couldn't shake the feeling that I had only scratched the surface of a much larger mystery—one that threatened to consume us both in its relentless pursuit of the truth.

In the quiet solitude of my thoughts, I found myself wrestling with conflicting emotions that seemed to pull me in opposite directions. There was this relentless sense of responsibility, a driving force urging me to uncover the truth and provide closure for John. It felt like a weight pressing down on my shoulders, demanding action and resolution.

But then there was this nagging doubt, a whisper of uncertainty that made me hesitate. What if I was wrong? What if my suspicions were unfounded, and I ended up causing more harm than good? The fear of making a mistake gnawed at me, casting shadows of doubt over my every thought.

Caught between these conflicting currents, I felt adrift, unsure of which path to follow. Should I trust my gut and pursue the truth, or should I hold back until I had solid evidence to support my suspicions? The uncertainty left me feeling paralyzed, unable to move forward without risking everything.

In the end, I knew I couldn't let fear dictate my actions. Despite the doubts swirling in my mind, I resolved to trust my instincts and pursue the truth, whatever it might uncover. It was a daunting prospect, filled with uncertainty and risk, but I couldn't ignore the call to uncover the secrets hidden beneath the surface.

## WHAT DO TERNS TASTE LIKE?

Heading off to work, I found myself lost in a haze of memories and regrets, my mind consumed by thoughts of Sara and Matt. It was only midway through the day that I realized Lisa had called me earlier, inviting me to dinner that evening. The prospect of spending time with her offered a glimmer of solace amidst the darkness that threatened to consume me, and I made a decision to pack up my work and leave the office early.

As the clock ticked closer to 5:30, I gathered my things and made my way out of the office, the weight of exhaustion pressing down on me like a leaden blanket. Determined to make the evening special, I stopped by a florist on the way, selecting a bouquet of fresh flowers to bring as a token of gratitude for Lisa's invitation. With the flowers in hand, I continued on my journey, the streets bustling with the hustle and bustle of evening commuters. The setting sun cast a warm glow over the city, bathing everything in a golden light as I made my way to Lisa's house. Despite the heaviness in my heart, there was a sense of anticipation building within me as I approached her front door. The thought of spending time with someone who cared about me offered a glimmer of hope in the midst of despair, a reminder that I was not alone in my grief.

Taking a deep breath, I rang the doorbell and waited, the sound echoing in the stillness of the evening. As the door swung open, I was greeted by the sight of Lisa's smiling face, her warmth washing over me like a wave as she welcomed me inside. "John, so glad you could make it!" she exclaimed, stepping aside to let me in. "Come on in, dinner's almost ready." I followed her inside, the warm scent of home-cooked food filling the air as I took in my surroundings. The living room was cozy and inviting, with plush sofas and soft lighting that cast a gentle glow over the room. Lisa's sister, Emily, sat on the couch, a book in hand as she greeted me with a friendly smile. "John, this is my sister, Emily," Lisa said, gesturing towards her. "Emily, this is John, the friend I was telling you about." Emily smiled warmly at me, setting her book aside as she rose to her feet. "It's nice to meet you, John," she said, extending her hand in greeting. "Lisa's told me so much about you." We chatted for a while, exchanging stories and getting to know each other better as we waited for dinner to be served. Emily was warm and engaging, her easy demeanor putting me at ease as we talked about everything from work to our hobbies and interests.

As we sat down to dinner, Lisa began to tell me more about her background, revealing that she was of Inuit descent*. I was intrigued, eager to learn more about her culture and heritage. "It's something I've always been proud of," Lisa explained, her eyes sparkling with pride. "Our traditions and customs have been passed down through generations, shaping who we are as a people."

Lisa got up and quickly made her way to the kitchen counter where there was a chicken-like dish prepared and served. She called out, "I have made something of an Inuit delicacy today for you John. These are Terns, and even though it might look a lot like chicken, you have to trust me that this tastes much better." The moment I heard Terns, my mind was transported back to the island, the memories flooding back with a force that left me reeling. I could vividly recall those days of desperation when Jake and I had scoured the island in search of food, our stomachs gnawing with hunger as we struggled to survive. It was Jake who had taken on the task of hunting the Terns, his determination driving him to brave the treacherous terrain in search of sustenance.

The image of Jake's face, grim and determined as he set out on his solitary hunts, flashed before my eyes, a stark reminder of the lengths we had gone to in order to stay alive. And as Lisa spoke of the Terns they had cooked for dinner, I couldn't shake the feeling of unease that settled in the pit of my stomach. The memories of those days on the island were still fresh in my mind, the taste of Terns lingering on my tongue like a bitter reminder of the hardships we had endured. And as we sat down to eat, the aroma of the cooked Terns filling the air, I found myself unable to stomach the thought of taking even a single bite. My mind was consumed by the memories of that time, the days of hunger and desperation etched into my very being. And as I looked around the table at the faces of those gathered, I couldn't help but wonder if they too understood the weight of what we had been through, the sacrifices we had made in order to survive.

As I tentatively took a bite of the cooked Tern meat, a wave of confusion washed over me. This was not what Tern tasted like back on the island. The flavor was different, almost unrecognizable, leaving me feeling disoriented and unsettled. Lisa and her sister looked on with concern, their brows furrowed in confusion as they watched my reaction. I could sense their unease, their puzzlement at my sudden change in demeanor. But I couldn't bring myself to explain, couldn't find the words to convey the tumult of emotions swirling within me.

Struggling to maintain my composure, I forced myself to continue eating, each bite a struggle against the rising tide of anger and frustration. This was not how it was supposed to be. This was not the taste of survival, of desperation and sacrifice. It was something else entirely, a pale imitation of the harsh reality we had faced on the island. Something didn't add up.

"Lisa, I have to ask," I began, my voice trembling with the weight of the questions that burned within me. "Where did you get the Terns from? Are there any nearby islands where you hunt these?" Lisa's expression faltered, a flicker of uncertainty crossing her features before she composed herself. "Oh, these Terns?" she replied, her tone casual but her eyes betraying a hint of apprehension. "They're actually imported from Canada. We don't have them anywhere close to our hometown."

Her words sent a chill down my spine, the pieces of the puzzle slotting into place with a sickening clarity. Imported from Canada? The realization hit me like a physical blow, leaving me reeling with a sense of betrayal. The realization struck me like a bolt of lightning: if these Terns were imported from Canada, then were there even any Terns on the island to begin with? Had Jake been lying to me all this time, spinning a web of deceit to keep me trapped in his twisted game? My heart hammered in my chest as I struggled to contain the rising tide of panic and anger that threatened to overwhelm me. I needed answers, and I needed them now.

As Lisa's response sank in, a wave of conflicting emotions washed over me, leaving me adrift in a sea of uncertainty and doubt. It was as if the pieces of a puzzle were finally falling into place, revealing a picture that I had been too blind to see before.

The realization hit me like a physical blow: Jake had been lying to me all along. The carefully constructed facade of our friendship crumbled before my eyes, revealing the cold, calculating manipulator lurking beneath. Every word, every action, every shared moment on that island suddenly took on a sinister hue, tainted by the knowledge that I had been deceived. How could Jake have done this to me? How could he have played me for a fool, exploiting my grief and vulnerability for his own twisted ends?

## LOOSE ENDS

The monotonous hum of the fluorescent lights buzzed in Detective Miller's ears, a relentless counterpoint to the storm brewing within him. Papers lay scattered across his desk, remnants of countless dead ends and frustrating leads. One thing Detective Mike knew was that he couldn't delay any longer. It was time to reach out to John and share with him the revelations I had uncovered, no matter how unsettling they might be. With trembling fingers, I dialed his number, my heart pounding in my chest as I waited for him to answer. After several rings, his voice came through the line, weary and strained.

"Hello?" he answered, his tone heavy with fatigue. "John, it's Mike," I said, my voice steady despite the turmoil raging within me. "I need to talk to you about something important." There was a brief pause on the other end of the line, the silence stretching between us like a taut wire. Then, with a heavy sigh, John spoke. "Sure, Mike," he replied, his voice tinged with resignation. "What is it?" Taking a deep breath to steady myself, I launched into an explanation of the discoveries I had made, recounting the inconsistencies in Jake's story and the troubling absence of evidence to support his claims. As I spoke, I could feel the tension mounting in the air, a palpable sense of unease that hung between us like a thick fog.

But before I could delve deeper into my findings, John interrupted me, his voice urgent and strained. "Mike, I need to tell you something," he said, his words tumbling out in a rush. "Something strange happened to me last night." Intrigued by his words, I leaned in closer, my curiosity piqued. "What happened?" I asked, my voice soft with concern. John proceeded to recount his experience at the dinner party, describing how he had been served a dish that purported to be Tern meat, only to discover that Terns did not inhabit the island where he and Jake had been stranded. As he spoke, I felt a chill run down my spine, the pieces of the puzzle clicking into place with alarming clarity.

"So you're saying that Jake lied about the Terns?" I asked, my mind racing with possibilities. John's response was a weary sigh, laden with resignation. "It certainly seems that way," he replied, his voice heavy with emotion. "And if he lied about that...what else has he been hiding?"

As the realization dawned on us, a heavy silence settled over the room, punctuated only by the sound of our ragged breaths. The implications of Jake's deception hung in the air like a dark cloud, casting a pall over our thoughts and emotions. John's voice trembled with anger as he struggled to contain the storm of emotions raging within him. "He used them... he used Sara and Matt," he whispered, his words choked with disbelief. "All this time... he was feeding us lies." The weight of his words bore down on me like a crushing weight, my mind reeling with the enormity of what we had uncovered. Anger surged through me like a raging inferno, threatening to consume me whole. "That son of a..." I began, my voice trailing off as I struggled to find the words to express my fury.

But before I could voice my outrage, John erupted in a torrent of rage, his voice rising to a crescendo of fury. "I want to kill him," he shouted, his words reverberating off the walls with chilling intensity. "I want to tear him apart with my bare hands." His words hung in the air like a solemn vow, a stark testament to the depths of his grief and anger. "John, you need to calm down." "We can't let our anger cloud our judgment. We need to find a way to get a confession out of him, to bring him to justice for what he's done." "I'm on my way to meet you," I assured John over the phone, my voice steady with determination. "Stay right where you are." John's response was a simple acknowledgment, but I could sense the gravity of his emotions through the line. As I hung up the phone and prepared to leave, a surge of adrenaline coursed through my veins. The weight of our mission hung heavy on my shoulders, but I knew that we couldn't afford to falter now.

∼

The phone clattered down on the receiver, the dial tone a shrill, mocking laugh in the sudden silence. Mike's words echoed in my skull, each syllable a hammer blow that shattered the fragile hope I'd been clinging to. The meat. Not tern. The truth, so monstrous and unthinkable, threatened to drown me in a wave of horror. The realization hit me like a ton of bricks – the meat we'd survived on during our time on the island wasn't from terns at all. It was something far more sinister, something I couldn't even bring myself to comprehend at first. The memories of those desperate days flooded back, each one now tainted by the horrifying truth. The laughter and smiles of Sara and Matt, once so precious to me, now seemed like cruel illusions, mocking reminders of what I'd lost.

Guilt gnawed at my insides as I grappled with the knowledge that I'd unknowingly consumed the flesh of my own family. How could I have been so blind, so oblivious to the truth right in front of me? But amidst the turmoil, a flicker of determination began to take hold. I couldn't let Jake get away with this – with what he'd done to Sara and Matt, to us. As Mike arrived, my emotions were in turmoil, my mind reeling from the horrifying revelation that Jake had been feeding me the flesh of my own wife and son. Anger surged within me like a raging inferno, fueled by disgust and betrayal.

"He fed me my own family, Mike!" I roared, my voice a ragged echo of the man I used to be. Tears welled in my eyes, hot and angry, blurring my vision. "My own wife and son! The sick son of a..." I couldn't finish the sentence. The words stuck in my throat, choked by a sob that tore through me. But the anger wouldn't be quelled. It burned in my gut, a white-hot inferno demanding release. "He deserves to die," I whispered, the words laced with a venom that surprised even me. "He deserves to rot in hell for what he's done!"

"I promise you, John," Mike said firmly, his voice cutting through the haze of my anger. "We will make sure Jake pays for what he's done. But we have to be smart about it. The best way to ensure he ends up behind bars is to catch him in the act." "We'll do this together, John," he continued, his gaze steady. "I'll be with you every step of the way. We'll get the evidence we need to put Jake away for good."

## THE FINAL DINNER

The evening sky hung heavy with the weight of impending dusk as I dialed Jake's number, my heart pounding in my chest with a mixture of anticipation and dread. With each ring, my nerves danced like wildfire, a flickering flame of uncertainty that threatened to engulf me whole. "Hey, Jake, it's John," I said, my voice steady despite the tumult raging within me. "I was thinking, how about we go out for dinner tonight? You know, to Le Bernardin, our favorite spot." There was a brief pause on the other end of the line, the silence stretching between us like a taut wire. I held my breath, waiting for Jake's response with bated anticipation. "Sure, sounds good," came his reply, his voice tinged with curiosity. "But what's the occasion? You never mentioned anything about dinner plans before." I hesitated for a moment, the weight of my words heavy on my tongue. "It's a surprise," I said finally, mustering a forced cheerfulness that belied the storm brewing within. "You'll find out when we get there." With a final exchange of pleasantries, we ended the call, leaving me alone with my thoughts and the gnawing sense of unease that lingered like a shadow in the depths of my mind.

Tears blurred my vision as I stood in front of the bathroom mirror, the weight of my grief pressing down on me like a suffocating blanket. Sara's laughter echoed in my mind, mingling with the innocent laughter of Matt as they danced together in my memory. How had it all come to this? How had our idyllic life been shattered by tragedy and betrayal? Taking a deep, shuddering breath, I wiped away the tears that streaked down my cheeks, willing myself to push aside the overwhelming tide of emotion threatening to consume me. Tonight was not about my pain, my loss—it was about justice, about closure. Steeling myself against the ache in my heart, I straightened my shoulders and composed myself, ready to face whatever lay ahead. Exiting the bathroom, I made my way back to the table, the din of the restaurant fading into the background as my thoughts turned inward once more. Mike's voice recorder lay hidden beneath my shirt, a silent witness to the events about to unfold. With each passing moment, the weight of its presence served as a reminder of the gravity of our mission, the importance of bringing Jake's deceit to light.

As the minutes ticked by, anticipation coiled tight in the pit of my stomach, my nerves thrumming with a mixture of apprehension and determination. The restaurant buzzed with activity, the clink of cutlery and murmur of conversation a distant backdrop to the tumult raging within me.

Finally, the moment arrived. Jake entered the restaurant, his familiar figure a stark contrast to the turmoil swirling within me. With a tight smile, I rose to greet him, my heart hammering in my chest as I ushered him to the table. The conversation flowed easily at first, a facade of normalcy masking the tension simmering beneath the surface. But as the evening wore on, I steered the conversation towards darker waters, towards the events that had torn our lives apart. With each word, Jake grew increasingly uneasy, his facade of nonchalance slipping away to reveal the flicker of fear in his eyes. His protests fell on deaf ears as I recounted the horrors of our time on the island, laying bare the truth of our ordeal for all to see. And then, the moment of reckoning arrived. With a dramatic flourish, I called for the special surprise I had arranged with the restaurant owner, the plate covered in cloche a symbol of the secrets waiting to be uncovered.

As the cloche was lifted, revealing the dish beneath, a hush fell over the table. Jake's eyes widened in shock, his face drained of color as he stared at the contents before him. Terns—succulent, juicy, and unmistakably familiar. A heavy silence hung in the air, broken only by the sound of our ragged breaths and the distant hum of the restaurant. In that moment, time seemed to stand still, the weight of our shared truth pressing down upon us like a leaden weight. And then, with a trembling hand, I reached for the voice recorder hidden beneath my shirt, its presence a silent testament to the lies that had bound us together. With a click, I activated the device, the sound of its recording echoing in the stillness of the room.

"Jake," I said, my voice steady despite the turmoil raging within me. "It's time to tell the truth." "This is what Terns taste like, Jake," I choked out between sobs, my voice thick with emotion. "What have you done with my wife and son? How could you do this to them?"

But Jake's response was swift, his words a cruel twist of the knife in my already wounded heart. "I did what I had to do so the both of us could survive on that island," he shouted back, his voice laced with desperation and defiance. "Your wife and son were already dead by the time I went to the other side of the island. I didn't kill them. But I had to use them so we could survive. Otherwise, none of us could survive that island for weeks." His words hung in the air, a damning confession that shattered the fragile semblance of normalcy that had enveloped us. Anger surged within me, a fiery tide that threatened to consume me whole. How could he justify his actions? How could he desecrate the memory of my beloved Sara and Matt with such callous disregard? But even as rage burned within me, a sense of resignation settled over me like a heavy cloak. The truth had been laid bare, the veil of deception torn apart. And as the weight of our shared reality pressed down upon us, I knew that there would be no turning back.

"This is all I needed to know," I whispered hoarsely, my voice barely audible above the din of the restaurant. With a heavy heart, I pushed back from the table, my legs trembling beneath me as I stumbled towards the exit. But Jake's voice echoed behind me, a desperate plea tinged with desperation. "Stop, John! Please, just listen to me!" he shouted, his words a frantic cacophony against the silence that enveloped us. But I paid his pleas no mind, my mind consumed by a single purpose: to seek justice for Sara and Matt, no matter the cost.

Rushing out into the cool night air, I made a beeline for my car, my hands shaking as I fumbled with the keys. The engine roared to life beneath me, the familiar hum of the motor a comforting embrace amidst the chaos that threatened to consume me. With a screech of tires, I peeled out of the parking lot, the road stretching out before me like an endless expanse of uncertainty. Tears blurred my vision as I raced towards the police station, my heart pounding in my chest with each passing moment. Arriving at last, I burst through the doors of the precinct, my breath ragged with exertion as I made my way to Mike's waiting figure. Without a word, I thrust the recording into his hands, my voice choked with emotion as I spoke. "It's done," I said, the weight of my words hanging heavy in the air between us.

Mike's eyes widened in surprise as he listened to the damning confession, his expression a mixture of shock and satisfaction. "You did it, John," he said, his voice filled with pride. "You got him."

## THE STORM

The day the restaurant erupted in chaos felt like a fever dream. One minute we were sharing a meal, the next, Mike was slapping cuffs on Jake and the world tilted on its axis. The man we'd clung to for survival, the one who'd spun a tale of shared struggle, was revealed as the monster behind the mask. It took a while, the legal gears grinding slow, but eventually charges were filed. Cannibalism. Murder. Life behind bars was still not fair enough for someone like Jake, but the justice system wasn't run on my will. As the days turned into weeks, and the weeks into months, the storm of turmoil that had raged within me gradually began to subside, leaving behind a quiet sense of calm in its wake. With Jake behind bars and Sara and Matt finally laid to rest, a weight had been lifted from my shoulders, the burden of grief and uncertainty replaced by a newfound sense of closure.

It was a crisp autumn morning when the news came, a phone call from Detective Mike informing me that a rescue party had been sent to the island and that Sara and Matt's remains had been found. Tears welled in my eyes as I listened to his words, a mixture of relief and sorrow washing over me like a tidal wave. With a heavy heart, I made my way to the morgue where their bodies had been brought, the air thick with the scent of antiseptic and mourning. Though their journey had been fraught with hardship and tragedy, they were finally home, their restless souls finding solace in the embrace of the earth. I let the morticians do their work, a strange detachment settling over me. It was like I was watching a movie, someone else's tragedy. Later, under a sky the color of faded denim, I stood by their freshly dug graves. The smell of damp earth mingled with the sweet fragrance of the lilies I placed on top. I sank down onto the rough wooden chair, the world a muted thrum around me.

As the days passed by, the emptiness within me seemed to grow, swallowing me whole in its relentless grip. Each morning brought with it a crushing sense of despair, the weight of my grief pressing down upon me like a suffocating blanket. I found myself adrift in a sea of sorrow, lost in a fog of memories that threatened to consume me whole. Caught in the grip of despair, my mind became a battlefield, torn between the desire to cling to the past and the need to find a way forward. Every moment seemed to stretch on endlessly, each breath a struggle against the tide of despair that threatened to drag me under. What was the point of it all, I wondered? What purpose did my life serve now that everything I held dear had been ripped away from me?

It was in the depths of this darkness that I made a decision, a choice born out of desperation and longing. With a heavy heart, I made my way to the cemetery, the weight of my sorrow pressing down upon me with each step. As I stood before the graves of Sara and Matt, my heart ached with a pain so profound it threatened to consume me whole. Tears welled in my eyes as I whispered my final goodbyes, the words catching in my throat as I struggled to find the strength to let go.

There was one last goodbye left to say, although it was an ugly one. The idea of seeing Jake festered in my gut, a bitter seed refusing to sprout. It wasn't some grand forgiveness I craved, no sudden urge to embrace the man who'd orchestrated our family's nightmare. It was exhaustion, a desperate yearning for a sliver of peace in the wreckage of my life. Staring at the crumpled permission slip in the cab, the official stamp mocked me. My hands trembled, slick with a nervous sweat that had nothing to do with the winter chill. Every fiber of my being screamed against this visit. Yet, a strange sense of duty, a morbid curiosity maybe, propelled me forward. The prison loomed, a hulking concrete monolith against the bruised winter sky. The sterile hallways echoed with every step, amplifying the hollowness that resonated within me. Finally, the visiting room. Sterile white walls and a scratched plexiglass barrier separated me from the man who now embodied my worst nightmares. Jake sat opposite, a gaunt figure swallowed by the drab orange jumpsuit.

Picking up the phone, the cold plastic felt alien against my skin. My mouth opened, but the words wouldn't come. I swallowed, the dryness in my throat a physical manifestation of the emotional turmoil. "I forgive you, Jake," I said, my voice barely above a whisper. "For everything that happened on that island, for everything that came after. I forgive you." Jake's eyes widened in surprise, his expression one of disbelief. "But why?" he asked, his voice tinged with confusion. "After everything I've done, how can you possibly forgive me?" I shook my head, a sad smile playing at the corners of my lips. "Because holding onto anger and resentment will only consume me from within," I replied. "I choose to let go, to find peace in forgiveness. It's the only way forward for both of us." Another shaky breath, locking eyes with Jake. "Forgiveness isn't for you, Jake," I said, each word a deliberate choice. "It's for me. It's a way to find some peace, to finally reach the ultimate chapter of my life."

I made my way out of the suffocating aura of the prison and approached the weather-beaten dock, my irregular footsteps and the tapping of the cane echoing against the worn wooden planks as I scanned the horizon for any sign of life. A lone fisherman tended to his boat, his weathered face creased with lines of concern as he glanced up at my approach. "Excuse me," I called out, my voice barely above a whisper as I approached the fisherman. "Could you...take me across the island, to the other side?" The fisherman regarded me with a mixture of curiosity and hesitation, his gaze lingering on the turbulent waters that lay beyond. "Are you sure about that, mate?" he asked, his voice tinged with a note of caution. "There's a storm brewing out there. Might not be the safest time to be out on the water." I nodded, my resolve firm despite the fisherman's warning. "I understand," I replied, my voice steady despite the turmoil churning within me. "But I need to do this. Please, will you take me?" "Name your price," I said, my voice surprisingly steady. The fisherman's eyes narrowed, a shrewd glint appearing within them. "Double the usual fare," he declared, watching my reaction. The amount was a hefty sum, enough to strain the already thin funds I had left. But the alternative – waiting, delaying this pilgrimage to the place where it all began – was unthinkable. Taking a deep breath, I reached into my pocket and pulled out my wallet. "Alright," I said, my voice hoarse. "Double it is. Just get me there as fast as this weather allows."

As the boat cut through the waves, I felt a sense of purpose wash over me, a quiet determination driving me forward despite the uncertainty that lay ahead. And as we sailed into the heart of the storm, I knew that whatever awaited me on the other side, I would face it with courage and conviction. Stepping onto the shore, I felt a sense of deja vu wash over me, the familiar sights and sounds of the island stirring long-forgotten memories within me. With each step, the sand shifted beneath my feet, a testament to the ever-changing nature of the world around me. But as I walked, I found solace in the rhythmic cadence of my footsteps, each one a step closer to the truth I sought.

As I wandered the shores of the island, I found myself drawn to the sea, its vast expanse stretching out before me like an endless expanse of possibility. The waves lapped gently at the shore, their rhythmic ebb and flow a soothing balm to my weary soul. But as I gazed out at the horizon, a sense of determination welled up within me, driving me forward despite the uncertainty that lay ahead.

With each step, the water grew deeper, the waves lapping at my ankles with increasing urgency. But I pressed on, driven by a sense of purpose that transcended words. As the water rose higher and higher, I felt a sense of liberation wash over me, a release from the burdens that had weighed me down for so long.

And as I waded deeper into the sea, the water rising up to my chest, I felt a profound sense of peace settle over me, a quiet acceptance of the journey that lay ahead. With one final breath, I let go of the past and embraced the future, knowing that whatever lay beyond the horizon, I would face it with courage and grace. The waves closed over my head and I felt a sense of freedom wash over me, the weight of the world lifting from my shoulders as I surrendered to the embrace of the sea. And in that moment, as the sun rose high in the sky, I knew that I had finally found the peace I had been searching for all along.

# THE END